Defoe Abbott Marx Hardy Montaigne Machiavelli Haggard Chesterton Cooper Emerson Joyce Austen Hugo Eliot Grimm
Melville Christie Maupassant Byron Molière Schiller
Stoker Carroll Wilde Garnett Fitzgerald Einstein Engels Smith Kafka Hall
Goethe Hawthorne Dostoyevsky Willis
Cotton Kipling Doyle
Baum Henry Nietzsche Balzac
Leslie Dumas Flaubert Turgenev Vatsyayana Crane
Stockton Verne Vinci
Burroughs Gogol Busch
Curtis Tocqueville Whitman
Homer Widger Tolstoy Twain Scott Plato Harte
Darwin Thoreau
Potter Freud Zola Lawrence Dickens Burton Hesse
Kant Jowett Stevenson Cervantes
Andersen Voltaire
London Descartes Cooke
Poe Aristotle Wells
Hale James Hastings Irving
Bunner Shakespeare
Richter Chambers da Chekhov Benedict Alcott
Doré Dante Shaw Pushkin
Swift Wodehouse Newton

Critical Miscellanies, Vol. I Essay 2: Carlyle

John Morley

Imprint

This book is part of TREDITION CLASSICS

Author: John Morley
Cover design: Buchgut, Berlin – Germany

Publisher: tredition GmbH, Hamburg - Germany
ISBN: 978-3-8472-3183-7

www.tredition.com
www.tredition.de

Copyright:
The content of this book is sourced from the public domain.

The intention of the TREDITION CLASSICS series is to make world literature in the public domain available in printed format. Literary enthusiasts and organizations, such as Project Gutenberg, worldwide have scanned and digitally edited the original texts. tredition has subsequently formatted and redesigned the content into a modern reading layout. Therefore, we cannot guarantee the exact reproduction of the original format of a particular historic edition. Please also note that no modifications have been made to the spelling, therefore it may differ from the orthography used today.

CARLYLE.

CARLYLE.

The new library edition of Mr. Carlyle's works may be taken for the final presentation of all that the author has to say to his contemporaries, and to possess the settled form in which he wishes his words to go to those of posterity who may prove to have ears for them. The canon is definitely made up. The golden Gospel of Silence is effectively compressed in thirty fine volumes. After all has been said about self-indulgent mannerisms, moral perversities, phraseological outrages, and the rest, these volumes will remain the noble monument of the industry, originality, conscientiousness, and genius of a noble character, and of an intellectual career that has exercised on many sides the profoundest sort of influence upon English feeling. Men who have long since moved far away from these spiritual latitudes, like those who still find an adequate shelter in them, can hardly help feeling as they turn the pages of the now disused pieces which they were once wont to ponder daily, that whatever later teachers may have done in definitely shaping opinion, in giving specific form to sentiment, and in subjecting [Pg 136] impulse to rational discipline, here was the friendly fire-bearer who first conveyed the Promethean spark, here the prophet who first smote the rock.

That with this sense of obligation to the master, there mixes a less satisfactory reminiscence of youthful excess in imitative phrases, in unseasonably apostolic readiness towards exhortation and rebuke, in interest about the soul, a portion of which might more profitably have been converted into care for the head, is in most cases true. A hostile observer of bands of Carlylites at Oxford and elsewhere might have been justified in describing the imperative duty of work as the theme of many an hour of strenuous idleness, and the superiority of golden silence over silver speech as the text of endless bursts of jerky rapture, while a too constant invective against cant had its usual effect of developing cant with a difference. To the incorrigibly sentimental all this was sheer poison, which continues tenaciously in the system. Others of robuster character no sooner came into contact with the world and its fortifying exigencies, than they at once began to assimilate the wholesome part of what they had taken in, while the rest falls gradually and silently out. When criticism has done its just work on the disagreeable affectations of many of Mr. Carlyle's disciples, and on the nature of Mr. Carlyle's opinions and their worth as specific contributions, very few people will be found to deny that his influence in stimulating moral energy, in kindling enthusiasm for virtues worthy of enthusiasm, [Pg 137] and in stirring a sense of the reality on the one hand, and the unreality on the other, of all that man can do or suffer, has not been surpassed by any teacher now living.

One of Mr. Carlyle's chief and just glories is, that for more than forty years he has clearly seen, and kept constantly and conspicuously in his own sight and that of his readers, the profoundly important crisis in the midst of which we are living. The moral and social dissolution in progress about us, and the enormous peril of sailing blindfold and haphazard, without rudder or compass or chart, have always been fully visible to him, and it is no fault of his if they have not become equally plain to his contemporaries. The policy of drifting has had no countenance from him. That a society should be likely to last with hollow and scanty faith, with no government, with a number of institutions hardly one of them real, with a horrible mass of poverty-stricken and hopeless subjects; that, if it should last, it could be regarded as other than an abomination of desolation, he has boldly and often declared to be things incredible. We are not promoting the objects which the social union subsists to fulfil, nor applying with energetic spirit to the task of preparing a sounder state for our successors. The relations between master and servant, between capitalist and labourer, between landlord and tenant, between governing race and subject race, between the feelings and intelligence of the legislature and the feelings [Pg 138] and intelligence of the nation, between the spiritual power, literary and ecclesiastical, and those who are under it—the anarchy that prevails in all these, and the extreme danger of it, have been with Mr. Carlyle a never-ending theme. What seems to many of us the extreme inefficiency or worse of his solutions, still allows us to feel grateful for the vigour and perspicacity with which he has pressed on the world the urgency of the problem.

The degree of durability which his influence is likely to possess with the next and following generations is another and rather sterile question, which we are not now concerned to discuss. The unrestrained eccentricities which Mr. Carlyle's strong individuality has precipitated in his written style may, in spite of the poetic fineness of his imagination, which no historian or humorist has excelled, still be expected to deprive his work of that permanence which is only secured by classic form. The incorporation of so many phrases, allusions, nicknames, that belong only to the hour, inevitably makes the vitality of the composition conditional on the vitality of these transient and accidental elements which are so deeply imbedded in it. Another consideration is that no philosophic writer, however ardently his words may have been treasured and followed by the people of his own time, can well be cherished by succeeding generations, unless his name is associated through some definable and positive contribution with the central march of European thought and [Pg 139] feeling. In other words, there is a difference between living in the history of literature or belief, and living in literature itself and in the minds of believers. Mr. Carlyle has been a most powerful solvent, but it is the tendency of solvents to become merely historic. The historian of the intellectual and moral movements of Great Britain during the present century, will fail egregiously in his task if he omits to give a large and conspicuous space to the author of *Sartor Resartus*. But it is one thing to study historically the ideas which have influenced our predecessors, and another thing to seek in them an influence fruitful for ourselves. It is to be hoped that one may doubt the permanent soundness of Mr. Carlyle's peculiar speculations, without either doubting or failing to share that warm affection and reverence which his personality has worthily inspired in many thousands of his readers. He has himself taught us to separate these two sides of a man, and we have learnt from him to love Samuel Johnson without reading much or a word that the old sage wrote. 'Sterling and I walked westward,' he says once, 'arguing copiously, but *except* in opinion not disagreeing.'

It is none the less for what has just been said a weightier and a rarer privilege for a man to give a stirring impulse to the moral activity of a generation, than to write in classic style; and to have impressed the spirit of his own personality deeply upon the minds of multitudes of men, than to have composed most of those works which the world is said not [Pg 140] willingly to let die. Nor, again, is to say that this higher renown belongs to Mr. Carlyle, to underrate the less resounding, but most substantial, services of a definite kind which he has rendered both to literature and history. This work may be in time superseded with the advance of knowledge, but the value of the first service will remain unimpaired. It was he, as has been said, 'who first taught England to appreciate Goethe;' and not only to appreciate Goethe, but to recognise and seek yet further knowledge of the genius and industry of Goethe's countrymen. His splendid drama of the French Revolution has done, and may be expected long to continue to do, more to bring before our slow-moving and unimaginative public the portentous meaning of that tremendous cataclysm, than all the other writings on the subject in the English language put together. His presentation of Puritanism and the Commonwealth and Oliver Cromwell first made the most elevating period of the national history in any way really intelligible. The Life of Frederick the Second, whatever judgment we may pass upon its morality, or even upon its place as a work of historic art, is a model of laborious and exhaustive narration of facts not before accessible to the reader of history. For all this, and for much other work eminently useful and meritorious even from the mechanical point of view, Mr. Carlyle deserves the warmest recognition. His genius gave him a right to mock at the ineffectiveness of Dryasdust, but his genius was also [Pg 141] too true to prevent him from adding the always needful supplement of a painstaking industry that rivals Dryasdust's own most strenuous toil. Take out of the mind of the English reader of ordinary cultivation and the average journalist, usually a degree or two lower than this, their conceptions of the French Revolution and the English Rebellion, and their knowledge of German literature and history, as well as most of their acquaintance with the prominent men of the eighteenth century, and we shall see how much work Mr. Carlyle has done simply as schoolmaster.

This, however, is emphatically a secondary aspect of his character, and of the function which he has fulfilled in relation to the more active tendencies of modern opinion and feeling. We must go on to other ground, if we would find the field in which he has laboured most ardently and with most acceptance. History and literature have been with him, what they will always be with wise and understanding minds of creative and even of the higher critical faculty—

only embodiments, illustrations, experiments, for ideas about religion, conduct, society, history, government, and all the other great heads and departments of a complete social doctrine. From this point of view, the time has perhaps come when we may fairly attempt to discern some of the tendencies which Mr. Carlyle has initiated or accelerated and deepened, though assuredly many years must elapse before any adequate measure can be taken of their force and final direction. [Pg 142]

It would be a comparatively simple process to affix the regulation labels of philosophy; to say that Mr. Carlyle is a Pantheist in religion (or a Pot-theist, to use the alternative whose flippancy gave such offence to Sterling on one occasion [1]), a Transcendentalist or Intuitionist in ethics, an Absolutist in politics, and so forth, with the addition of a crowd of privative or negative epithets at discretion. But classifications of this sort are the worst enemies of true knowledge. Such names are by the vast majority even of persons who think themselves educated, imperfectly apprehended, ignorantly interpreted, and crudely and recklessly applied. It is not too much to say that nine out of ten people who think they have delivered themselves of a criticism when they call Mr. Carlyle a Pantheist, could neither explain with any precision what Pantheism is, nor have ever thought of determining the parts of his writings where this particular monster is believed to lurk. Labels are devices for saving talkative persons the trouble of thinking. As I once wrote elsewhere:

'The readiness to use general names in speaking of the greater subjects, and the fitness which qualifies a man to use them, commonly exist in inverse proportions. If we reflect on the conditions out of which ordinary opinion is generated, we may well be startled at the profuse liberality with which names of the widest and most complex and variable significance are bestowed on all hands. The majority of [Pg 143] the ideas which constitute most men's intellectual stock-in-trade have accrued by processes quite distinct from fair reasoning and consequent conviction. This is so notorious, that it is amazing how so many people can go on freely and rapidly labelling thinkers or writers with names which they themselves are not competent to bestow, and which their hearers are not competent either to understand generally, or to test in the specific instance.'

These labels are rather more worthless than usual in the present case, because Mr. Carlyle is ostentatiously illogical and defiantly inconsistent; and, therefore, the term which might correctly describe one side of his teaching or belief would be tolerably sure to give a wholly false impression of some of its other sides. The qualifications necessary to make any one of the regular epithets fairly applicable would have to be so many, that the glosses would virtually overlay the text. We shall be more likely to reach an instructive appreciation by discarding such substitutes for examination, and considering, not what pantheistic, absolutist, transcendental, or any other doctrine means, or what it is worth, but what it is that Mr. Carlyle means about men, their character, their relations to one another, and what that is worth.

With most men and women the master element in their opinions is obviously neither their own reason nor their own imagination, independently exercised, but only mere use and wont, chequered by fortuitous [Pg 144] sensations, and modified in the better cases by the influence of a favourite teacher; while in the worse the teacher is the favourite who happens to chime in most harmoniously with prepossessions, or most effectually to nurse and exaggerate them. Among the superior minds the balance between reason and imagination is scarcely ever held exactly true, nor is either firmly kept within the precise bounds that are proper to it. It is a question of temperament which of the two mental attitudes becomes fixed and habitual, as it is a question of temperament how violently either of them straitens and distorts the normal faculties of vision. The man who prides himself on a hard head, which would usually be better described as a thin head, may and constantly does fall into a confirmed manner of judging character and circumstance, so narrow, one-sided, and elaborately superficial, as to make common sense shudder at the crimes that are committed in the divine name of reason. Excess on the other side leads people into emotional transports, in which the pre-eminent respect that is due to truth, the difficulty of discovering the truth, the narrowness of the way that leads thereto, the merits of intellectual precision and definiteness, and even the merits of moral precision and definiteness, are all effectually veiled by purple or fiery clouds of anger, sympathy, and sentimentalism, which imagination has hung over the intelligence.

The familiar distinction between the poetic and the scientific temper is another way of stating the same [Pg 145] difference. The one fuses or crystallises external objects and circumstances in the medium of human feeling and passion; the other is concerned with the relations of objects and circumstances among themselves, including in them all the facts of human consciousness, and with the discovery and classification of these relations. There is, too, a corresponding distinction between the aspects which conduct, character, social movement, and the objects of nature are able to present, according as we scrutinise them with a view to exactitude of knowledge, or are stirred by some appeal which they make to our various faculties and forms of sensibility, our tenderness, sympathy, awe, terror, love of beauty, and all the other emotions in this momentous catalogue. The starry heavens have one side for the astronomer, as astronomer, and another for the poet, as poet. The nightingale, the skylark, the cuckoo, move one sort of interest in an ornithologist, and a very different sort in a Shelley or a Wordsworth. The hoary and stupendous formations of the inorganic world, the thousand tribes of insects, the great universe of plants, from those whose size and form and hue make us afraid as if they were deadly monsters, down to 'the meanest flower that blows,' all these are clothed with one set of attributes by scientific intelligence, and with another by sentiment, fancy, and imaginative association.

The contentiousness of rival schools of philosophy has obscured the application of the same distinction to the various orders of fact more nearly and immedi [Pg 146] ately relating to man and the social union. One school has maintained the virtually unmeaning doctrine that the will is free, and therefore its followers never gave any quarter to the idea that man was as proper an object of scientific scrutiny morally and historically, as they could not deny him to be anatomically and physiologically. Their enemies have been more concerned to dislodge them from this position, than to fortify, organise, and cultivate their own. The consequences have not been without their danger. Poetic persons have rushed in where scientific persons ought not to have feared to tread. That human character and the order of events have their poetic aspect, and that their poetic treatment demands the rarest and most valuable qualities of mind, is a truth which none but narrow and superficial men of the world are rash enough to deny. But that there is a scientific aspect of these things, an order among them that can only be understood and criticised and effectually modified scientifically, by using all the caution and precision and infinite patience of the truly scientific spirit, is a truth that is constantly ignored even by men and women of the loftiest and most humane nature. In such cases misdirected and uncontrolled sensibility ends in mournful waste of their own energy, in the certain disappointment of their own aims, and where such sensibility is backed by genius, eloquence, and a peculiar set of public conditions, in prolonged and fatal disturbance of society.

Rousseau was the great type of this triumphant and [Pg 147] dangerous sophistry of the emotions. The Rousseau of these times for English-speaking nations is Thomas Carlyle. An apology is perhaps needed for mentioning a man of such simple, veracious, disinterested, and wholly high-minded life, in the same breath with one of the least sane men that ever lived. Community of method, like misery, makes men acquainted with strange bed-fellows. Two men of very different degrees of moral worth may notoriously both preach the same faith and both pursue the same method, and the method of Rousseau is the method of Mr. Carlyle. With each of them thought is an aspiration, and justice a sentiment, and society a retrogression. Each bids us look within our own bosoms for truth and right, postpones reason, to feeling, and refers to introspection and a factitious something styled Nature, questions only to be truly solved by external observation and history. In connection with each of them has been exemplified the cruelty inherent in sentimentalism, when circumstances draw away the mask. Not the least conspicuous of the disciples of Rousseau was Robespierre. His works lay on the table of the Committee of Public Safety. The theory of the Reign of Terror was invented, and mercilessly reduced to practice, by men whom the visions of Rousseau had fired, and who were not afraid nor ashamed to wade through oceans of blood to the promised land of humanity and fine feeling. We in our days have seen the same result of sentimental doctrine in the barbarous love of the battle-field, the retrograde [Pg 148] passion for methods of repression, the contempt for human life, the impatience of orderly and peaceful solution. We begin with introspection and the eternities, and end in blood and iron. Again, Rousseau's first piece was an anathema upon the science and art of his time, and a denunciation of books and speech. Mr. Carlyle, in exactly the same spirit, has denounced logic mills, warned us all away from literature, and habitually subordinated discipline of the intelligence to the passionate assertion of the will. There are passages in which he speaks respectfully of Intellect, but he is always careful to show that he is using the term in a special sense of his own, and confounding it with 'the exact summary of human *Worth*,' as in one place he defines it. Thus, instead of co-ordinating moral worthiness with intellectual energy, virtue with intelligence, right action of the will with scientific processes of the understanding, he has either placed one immeasurably below the other, or else has mischievously insisted on treating them as identical. The dictates of a kind heart are of superior force to the maxims of political economy; swift and peremptory resolution is a safer guide than a balancing judgment. If the will works easily and surely, we may assume the rectitude of the moving impulse. All this is no caricature of a system which sets sentiment, sometimes hard sentiment and sometimes soft sentiment, above reason and method.

In other words, the writer who in these days has done more than anybody else to fire men's hearts [Pg 149] with a feeling for right and an eager desire for social activity, has with deliberate contempt thrust away from him the only instruments by which we can make sure what right is, and that our social action is wise and effective. A born poet, only wanting perhaps a clearer feeling for form and a more delicate spiritual self-possession, to have added another name to the illustrious catalogue of English singers, he has been driven by the impetuosity of his sympathies to attack the scientific side of social questions in an imaginative and highly emotional manner. Depth of benevolent feeling is unhappily no proof of fitness for handling complex problems, and a fine sense of the picturesque is no more a qualification for dealing effectively with the difficulties of an old society, than the composition of Wordsworth's famous sonnet on Westminster Bridge was any reason for supposing that the author would have made a competent Commissioner of Works.

Why should society, with its long and deep-hidden processes of growth, its innumerable intricacies and far-off historic complexities, be as an open book to any reader of its pages who brings acuteness and passion, but no patience nor calm accuracy of meditation? Objects of thought and observation far simpler, more free from all blinding and distorting elements, more accessible to direct and ocular inspection, are by rational consent reserved for the calmest and most austere moods and methods of human intelligence. Nor is denunciation of the [Pg 150] conditions of a problem the quickest step towards solving it. Vituperation of the fact that supply and demand practically regulate certain kinds of bargain, is no contribution to systematic efforts to discover some more moral regulator. Take all the invective that Mr. Carlyle has poured out against political economy, the Dismal Science, and Gospel according to M'Croudy. Granting the absolute and entire inadequateness of political economy to sum up the laws and conditions of a healthy social state—and no one more than the present writer deplores the mischief which the application of the maxims of political economy by ignorant and selfish spirits has effected in confirming the worst tendencies of the commercial character—yet is it not a first condition of our being able to substitute better machinery for the ordinary rules of self-interest, that we know scientifically how those rules do and must operate? Again, in another field, it is well to cry out: 'Caitiff, we hate thee,' with a 'hatred, a hostility inexorable, unappeasable, which blasts the scoundrel, and all scoundrels ultimately, into black annihilation and disappearance from the scene of things.' [2] But this is slightly vague. It is not scientific. There are caitiffs and caitiffs. There is a more and a less of scoundrelism, as there is a more and a less of black annihilation, and we must have systematic jurisprudence, with its classification of caitiffs and its graduated blasting. Has Mr. Carlyle's passion, or [Pg 151] have the sedulous and scientific labours of that Bentham, whose name with him is a symbol of evil, done most in what he calls the Scoundrel-province of Reform within the last half-century? Sterling's criticism on Teufelsdröckh told a hard but wholesome truth to Teufelsdröckh's creator. 'Wanting peace himself,' said Sterling, 'his fierce dissatisfaction fixes on all that is weak, corrupt, and imperfect around him; and instead of a calm and steady co-operation with all those who are endeavouring to apply the highest ideas as remedies for the worst evils, he holds himself in savage isolation.' [3]

Mr. Carlyle assures us of Bonaparte that he had an instinct of nature better than his culture was, and illustrates it by the story that during the Egyptian expedition, when his scientific men were busy arguing that there could be no God, Bonaparte, looking up to the stars, confuted them decisively by saying: 'Very ingenious, Messieurs; but *who made* all that?' Surely the most inconclusive answer since coxcombs vanquished Berkeley with a grin. It is, however, a type of Mr. Carlyle's faith in the instinct of nature, as superseding the necessity for patient logical method; a faith, in other words, in crude and uninterpreted sense. Insight, indeed, goes far, but it no more entitles its possessor to dispense with reasoned discipline and system in treating scientific subjects, than it relieves him from the necessity of conforming to the physical conditions of health. Why should [Pg 152] society be the one field of thought in which a man of genius is at liberty to assume all his major premisses, and swear all his conclusions?

The deep unrest of unsatisfied souls meets its earliest solace in the effective and sympathetic expression of the same unrest from the lips of another. To look it in the face is the first approach to a sedative. To find our discontent with the actual, our yearning for an undefined ideal, our aspiration after impossible heights of being, shared and amplified in the emotional speech of a man of genius, is the beginning of consolation. Some of the most generous spirits a hundred years ago found this in the eloquence of Rousseau, and some of the most generous spirits of this time and place have found it in the writer of the *Sartor*. In ages not of faith, there will always be multitudinous troops of people crying for the moon. If such sorrowful pastime be ever permissible to men, it has been natural and lawful this long while in præ-revolutionary England, as it was natural and lawful a century since in præ-revolutionary France. A man born into a community where political forms, from the monarchy down to the popular chamber, are mainly hollow shams disguising the coarse supremacy of wealth, where religion is mainly official and political, and is ever too ready to dissever itself alike from the spirit of justice, the spirit of charity, and the spirit of truth, and where literature does not as a rule permit itself to discuss serious subjects frankly [Pg 153] and worthily [4] — a community, in short, where the great aim of all classes and orders with power is by dint of rigorous silence, fast shutting of the eyes, and stern stopping of the ears, somehow to keep the social pyramid on its apex, with the fatal result of preserving for England its glorious fame as a paradise for the well-to-do, a purgatory for the able, and a hell for the poor—why, a man born into all this with a heart something softer than a flint, and with intellectual vision something more acute than that of a Troglodyte, may well be allowed to turn aside and cry for moons for a season.

Impotent unrest, however, is followed in Mr. Carlyle by what is socially an impotent solution, just as it was with Rousseau. To bid a man do his duty in one page, and then in the next to warn him sternly away from utilitarianism, from political economy, from all 'theories of the moral sense,' and from any other definite means of ascertaining what duty may chance to be, is but a bald and naked counsel. Spiritual nullity and material confusion in a society are not to be repaired by a transformation of egotism, querulous, brooding, marvelling, into egotism, active, practical, objective, not uncomplacent. The moral movements to which the instinctive impulses of humanity fallen on evil times uniformly give birth, early Christianity, for instance, or the socialism of Rousseau, may destroy a society, but they cannot save it unless in conjunction with organising policy. A thorough [Pg 154] appreciation of fiscal and economic truths was at least as indispensable for the life of the Roman Empire as the acceptance of a Messiah; and it was only in the hands of a great statesman like Gregory VII. that Christianity became at last an instrument powerful enough to save civilisation. What the moral renovation of Rousseau did for France we all know. Now Rousseau's was far more profoundly social than the doctrine of Mr. Carlyle, which, while in name a renunciation of self, has all its foundations in the purest individualism. Rousseau, notwithstanding the method of *Emile*, treats man as a part of a collective whole, contracting manifold relations and owing manifold duties; and he always appeals to the love and sympathy which an imaginary God of nature has implanted in the heart. His aim is unity. Mr. Carlyle, following the same method of obedience to his own personal emotions, unfortified by patient reasoning, lands at the other extremity, and lays all his stress on the separatist instincts. The individual stands alone confronted by the eternities; between these and his own soul exists the one central relation. This has all the fundamental egotism of the doctrine of personal salvation, emancipated from fable, and varnished with an emotional phrase. The doctrine has been very widely interpreted, and without any forcing, as a religious expression for the conditions of commercial success.

If we look among our own countrymen, we find that the apostle of self-renunciation is nowhere so [Pg 155] beloved as by the best of those whom steady self-reliance and thrifty self-securing and a firm eye to the main chance have got successfully on in the world. A Carlylean anthology, or volume of the master's sentences, might easily be composed, that should contain the highest form of private liturgy accepted by the best of the industrial classes, masters or men. They forgive or overlook the writer's denunciations of Beaver Industrialisms, which they attribute to his caprice or spleen. This is the worst of an emotional teacher, that people take only so much as they please from him, while with a reasoner they must either refute by reason, or else they must accept by reason, and not at simple choice. When trade is brisk, and England is successfully competing in the foreign markets, the books that enjoin silence and self-annihilation have a wonderful popularity in the manufacturing districts. This circumstance is honourable both to them and to him, as far as it goes, but it furnishes some reason for suspecting that our most vigorous moral reformer, so far from propelling us in new grooves, has in truth only given new firmness and coherency to tendencies that were strongly marked enough in the national character before. He has increased the fervour of the country, but without materially changing its objects; there is all the less disguise among us as a result of his teaching, but no radical modification of the sentiments which people are sincere in. The most stirring general appeal to the emotions, to be effective for [Pg 156] more than negative purposes, must lead up to definite maxims and specific precepts. As a negative renovation Mr. Carlyle's doctrine was perfect. It effectually put an end to the mood of Byronism. May we say that with the neutralisation of Byron, his most decisive and special work came to an end? May we not say further, that the true renovation of England, if such a process be ever feasible, will lie in a quite other method than this of emotion? It will lie not in more moral earnestness only, but in a more open intelligence; not merely in a more dogged resolution to work and be silent, but in a ready willingness to use the understanding. The poison of our sins, says Mr.

Carlyle in his latest utterance, 'is not intellectual dimness chiefly, but torpid unveracity of heart.' Yes, but all unveracity, torpid or fervid, breeds intellectual dimness, and it is this last which prevents us from seeing a way out of the present ignoble situation. We need light more than heat; intellectual alertness, faith in the reasoning faculty, accessibility to new ideas. To refuse to use the intellect patiently and with system, to decline to seek scientific truth, to prefer effusive indulgence of emotion to the laborious and disciplined and candid exploration of new ideas, is not this, too, a torpid unveracity? And has not Mr. Carlyle, by the impatience of his method, done somewhat to deepen it?

It is very well to invite us to moral reform, to bring ourselves to be of heroic mind, as the surest way to 'the blessed Aristocracy of the Wisest.' But how shall we know the wisest when we see them, and [Pg 157] how shall a nation know, if not by keen respect and watchfulness for intellectual truth and the teachers of it? Much as we may admire Mr. Carlyle's many gifts, and highly as we may revere his character, it is yet very doubtful whether anybody has as yet learnt from him the precious lesson of scrupulosity and conscientiousness in actively and constantly using the intelligence. This would have been the solid foundation of the true hero-worship.

Let thus much have been said on the head of temperament. The historic position also of every writer is an indispensable key to many things in his teaching. [5] We have to remember in Mr. Carlyle's case, that he was born in the memorable year when the French Revolution, in its narrower sense, was closed by the Whiff of Grapeshot, and when the great century of emancipation and illumination was ending darkly in battles and confusion. During his youth the reaction was in full flow, and the lamp had been handed to runners who not only reversed the ideas and methods, but even turned aside from the goal of their precursors. Hopefulness and enthusiastic confidence in humanity when freed from the fetters of spiritual superstition and secular tyranny, marked all the most characteristic and influential speculations [Pg 158] of the two generations before '89. The appalling failure which attended the splendid attempt to realise these hopes in a renewed and perfected social structure, had no more than its natural effect in turning men's minds back, not to the past of Rousseau's imagination, but to the past of recorded history. The single epoch in the annals of Europe since the rise of Christianity, for which no good word could be found, was the epoch of Voltaire. The hideousness of the Christian church in the ninth and tenth centuries was passed lightly over by men who had only eyes for the moral obliquity of the church of the Encyclopædia. The brilliant but profoundly inadequate essays on Voltaire and Diderot were the outcome in Mr. Carlyle of the same reactionary spirit. Nobody now, we may suppose, who is competent to judge, thinks that that estimate of 'the net product, of the tumultuous Atheism' of Diderot and his fellow-workers, is a satisfactory account of the influence and significance of the Encyclopædia; nor that to sum up Voltaire, with his burning passion for justice, his indefatigable humanity, his splendid energy in intellectual production, his righteous hatred of superstition, as merely a supreme master of *persiflage*, can be a process partaking of finality. The fact that to the eighteenth century belong the subjects of more than half of these thirty volumes, is a proof of the fascination of the period for an author who has never ceased to vilipend it. The saying is perhaps as true in these matters as of private relations, that hatred is not so [Pg 159] far removed from love as indifference is. Be that as it may, the Carlylean view of the eighteenth century as a time of mere scepticism and unbelief, is now clearly untenable to men who remember the fervour of Jean Jacques, and the more rational, but not any less fervid faith of the disciples of Perfectibility. But this was not so clear fifty years since, when the crash and dust of demolition had not so subsided as to let men see how much had risen up behind. The fire of the new school had been taken from the very conflagration which they execrated, but they were not held back from denouncing the eighteenth century by the reflection that, at any rate, its thought and action had made ready the way for much of what is best in the nineteenth.

Mr. Carlyle himself has told us about Coleridge, and the movement of which Coleridge was the leader. That movement has led men in widely different ways. In one direction it has stagnated in the sunless swamps of a theosophy, from which a cloud of sedulous ephemera still suck a little spiritual moisture. In another it led to the sacramental and sacerdotal developments of Anglicanism. In a third, among men with strong practical energy, to the benevolent bluster of a sort of Christianity which is called muscular because it is not intellectual. It would be an error to suppose that these and the other streams that have sprung from the same source, did not in the days of their fulness fertilise and gladden many lands. The wordy pietism of one school, the mimetic rites of [Pg 160] another, the romping heroics of the third, are degenerate forms. How long they are likely to endure, it would be rash to predict among a nation whose established teachers and official preachers are prevented by an inveterate timidity from trusting themselves to that disciplined intelligence, in which the superior minds of the last century had such courageous faith.

Mr. Carlyle drank in some sort at the same fountain. Coleridgean ideas were in the air. It was there probably that he acquired that sympathy with the past, or with certain portions of the past, that feeling of the unity of history, and that conviction of the necessity of binding our theory of history fast with our theory of other things, in all of which he so strikingly resembles the great Anglican leaders of a generation ago, and in gaining some of which so strenuous an effort must have been needed to modify the prepossessions of a Scotch Puritan education. No one has contributed more powerfully to that movement which, drawing force from many and various sides, has brought out the difference between the historian and the gazetteer or antiquary. One half of *Past and Present* might have been written by one of the Oxford chiefs in the days of the Tracts. Vehement native force was too strong for such a man to remain in the luminous haze which made the Coleridgean atmosphere. A well-known chapter in the *Life of Sterling*, which some, indeed, have found too ungracious, shows how little hold he felt Coleridge's [Pg 161] ideas to be capable of retaining, and how little permanent satisfaction resided in them. Coleridge, in fact, was not only a poet but a thinker as well; he had science of a sort as well as imagination, but it was not science for headlong and impatient souls. Mr. Carlyle has probably never been able to endure a subdivision all his life, and the infinite ramifications of the central division between object and subject might well be with him an unprofitable weariness to the flesh.

In England, the greatest literary organ of the Revolution was unquestionably Byron, whose genius, daring, and melodramatic lawlessness, exercised what now seems such an amazing fascination over the least revolutionary of European nations. Unfitted for scientific work and full of ardour, Mr. Carlyle found his mission in rushing with all his might to the annihilation of this terrible poet, who, like some gorgon, hydra, or chimera dire planted at the gate, carried off a yearly tale of youths and virgins from the city. In literature, only a revolutionist can thoroughly overpower a revolutionist. Mr. Carlyle had fully as much daring as Byron; his writing at its best, if without the many-eyed minuteness and sustained pulsing force of Byron, has still the full swell and tide and energy of genius: he is as lawless in his disrespect for some things established. He had the unspeakable advantage of being that which, though not in this sense, only his own favourite word of contempt describes, respectable; and, for another thing, [Pg 162] of being ruggedly sincere. Carlylism is the male of Byronism. It is Byronism with thew and sinew, bass pipe and shaggy bosom. There is the same grievous complaint against the time and its men and its spirit, something even of the same contemptuous despair, the same sense of the puniness of man in the centre of a cruel and frowning universe; but there is in Carlylism a deliverance from it all, indeed the only deliverance possible. Its despair is a despair without misery. Labour in a high spirit, duty done, and right service performed in fortitudinous temper — here was, not indeed a way out, but a way of erect living within.

Against Byronism the ordinary moralist and preacher could really do nothing, because Byronism was an appeal that lay in the regions of the mind only accessible by one with an eye and a large poetic feeling for the infinite whole of things. It was not the rebellion only in *Manfred*, nor the wit in *Don Juan*, nor the graceful melancholy of *Childe Harold*, which made their author an idol, and still make him one to multitudes of Frenchmen and Germans and Italians. One prime secret of it is the air and spaciousness, the freedom and elemental grandeur of Byron. Who has not felt this to be one of the glories of Mr. Carlyle's work, that it, too, is large and spacious, rich with the fulness of a sense of things unknown and wonderful, and ever in the tiniest part showing us the stupendous and overwhelming whole? The magnitude of the universal forces enlarges the pettiness of man, and the smallness of his achievement and endurance takes a complexion [Pg 163] of greatness from the vague immensity that surrounds and impalpably mixes with it.

Remember further, that while in Byron the outcome of this was rebellion, in Carlyle its outcome is reverence, a noble mood, which is one of the highest predispositions of the English character. The instincts of sanctification rooted in Teutonic races, and which in the corrupt and unctuous forms of a mechanical religious profession are so revolting, were mocked and outraged, where they were not superciliously ignored, in every line of the one, while in the other they were enthroned under the name of Worship, as the very key and centre of the right life. The prophet who never wearies of declaring that 'only in bowing down before the Higher does man feel himself exalted,' touched solemn organ notes, that awoke a response from dim religious depths, never reached by the stormy wailings of the Byronic lyre. The political side of the reverential sentiment is equally conciliated, and the prime business of individuals and communities pronounced to be the search after worthy objects of this divine quality of reverence. While kings' cloaks and church tippets are never spared, still less suffered to protect the dishonour of ignoble wearers of them, the inadequateness of aggression and demolition, the necessity of quiet order, the uncounted debt that we owe to rulers and to all sorts of holy and great men who have given this order to the world, all this brought repose and harmony into spirits that the hollow thunders of universal rebellion against tyrants and priests had [Pg 164] worn into thinness and confusion. Again, at the bottom of the veriest *frondeur* with English blood in his veins, in his most defiant moment there lies a conviction that after all something known as common sense is the measure of life, and that to work hard is a demonstrated precept of common sense. Carlylism exactly hits this and brings it forward. We cannot wonder that Byronism was routed from the field.

It may have been in the transcendently firm and clear-eyed intelligence of Goethe that Mr. Carlyle first found a responsive encouragement to the profoundly positive impulses of his own spirit. [6] There is, indeed, a whole heaven betwixt the serenity, balance, and bright composure of the one, and the vehemence, passion, masterful wrath, of the other; and the vast, incessant, exact inquisitiveness of Goethe finds nothing corresponding to it in Mr. Carlyle's multitudinous contempt and indifference, sometimes express and sometimes only very significantly implied, for forms of intellectual activity that do not happen to be personally congenial. But each is a god, though the one sits ever on Olympus, while the other is as one from Tartarus. There is in each, besides all else, a [Pg 165] certain remarkable directness of glance, an intrepid and penetrating quality of vision, which defies analysis. Occasional turgidity of phrase and unidiomatic handling of language do not conceal the simplicity of the process by which Mr. Carlyle pierces through obstruction down to the abstrusest depths. And the important fact is that this abstruseness is not verbal, any more than it is the abstruseness of fog and cloud. His epithet, or image, or trope, shoots like a sunbeam on to the matter, throwing a transfigurating light, even where it fails to pierce to its central core.

Eager for a firm foothold, yet wholly revolted by the too narrow and unelevated positivity of the eighteenth century; eager also for some recognition of the wide realm of the unknowable, yet wholly unsatisfied by the transcendentalism of the English and Scotch philosophic reactions; he found in Goethe that truly free and adequate positivity which accepts all things as parts of a natural or historic order, and while insisting on the recognition of the actual conditions of this order as indispensable, and condemning attempted evasions of such recognition as futile and childish, yet opens an ample bosom for all forms of beauty in art, and for all nobleness in moral aspiration. That Mr. Carlyle has reached this high ground we do not say. Temperament has kept him down from it. But it is after this that he has striven. The tumid nothingness of pure transcendentalism he has always abhorred. Some of Mr. Carlyle's favourite phrases have disguised from his readers the intensely practical [Pg 166] turn of his whole mind. His constant presentation of the Eternities, the Immensities, and the like, has veiled his almost narrow adherence to plain record without moral comment, and his often cynical respect for the dangerous, yet, when rightly qualified and guided, the solid formula that What is, is. The Eternities and Immensities are only a kind of awful background. The highest souls are held to be deeply conscious of these vast unspeakable presences, yet even with them they are only inspiring accessories; the true interest lies in the practical attitude of such men towards the actual and palpable circumstances that surround them. This spirituality, whose place in Mr. Carlyle's teaching has been so extremely mis-stated, sinks wholly out of sight in connection with such heroes as the coarse and materialist Bonaparte, of whom, however, the hero-worshipper in earlier pieces speaks with some laudable misgiving, and the not less coarse and materialist Frederick, about whom no misgiving is permitted to the loyal disciple. The admiration for military methods, on condition that they are successful, for Mr. Carlyle, like Providence, is always on the side of big and victorious battalions, is the last outcome of a devotion to vigorous action and practical effect, which no verbal garniture of a transcendental kind can hinder us from perceiving to be more purely materialist and unfeignedly brutal than anything which sprung from the reviled thought of the eighteenth century.

It is instructive to remark that another of the most [Pg 167] illustrious enemies of that century and all its works, Joseph de Maistre, had the same admiration for the effectiveness of war, and the same extreme interest and concern in the men and things of war. He, too, declares that 'the loftiest and most generous sentiments are probably to be found in the soldier;' and that war, if terrible, is divine and splendid and fascinating, the manifestation of a sublime law of the universe. We must, however, do De Maistre the justice to point out, first, that he gave a measure of his strange interest in Surgery and Judgment, as Mr. Carlyle calls it, to the public executioner, a division of the honours of social surgery which is no more than fair; while, in the second place, he redeems the brutality of the military surgical idea after a fashion, by an extraordinary mysticism, which led him to see in war a divine, inscrutable force, determining success in a manner absolutely defying all the speculations of human reason. [7] The biographer of Frederick apparently finds no inscrutable force at all, but only will, tenacity, and powder kept dry. There is a vast difference between this and the absolutism of the mystic.

'Nature,' he says in one place, 'keeps silently a most exact Savings-bank, and official register correct to the most evanescent item, Debtor and Creditor, in respect to one and all of us; silently marks down, Creditor by such and such an unseen act of veracity and heroism; Debtor to such a loud blustery blunder, [Pg 168] twenty-seven million strong or one unit strong, and to all acts and words and thoughts executed in consequence of that—Debtor, Debtor, Debtor, day after day, rigorously as Fate (for this *is* Fate that is writing); and at the end of the account you will have it all to pay, my friend.' [8]

That is to say, there is a law of recompense for communities of men, and as nations sow, even thus they reap. But what is Mr. Carlyle's account of the precise nature and operation of this law? What is the original distinction between an act of veracity and a blunder? Why was the blow struck by the Directory on the Eighteenth Fructidor a blunder, and that struck by Bonaparte on the Eighteenth Brumaire a veracity? What principle of registration is that which makes Nature debtor to Frederick the Second for the seizure of Silesia, and Bonaparte debtor to Nature for 'trampling on the world, holding it tyrannously down?' It is very well to tell us that 'Injustice pays itself with frightful compound interest,' but there are reasons for suspecting that Mr. Carlyle's definition of the just and the unjust are such as to reduce this and all his other sentences of like purport to the level of mere truism and repetition. If you secretly or openly hold that to be just and veracious which is successful, then it needs no further demonstration that penalties of ultimate failure are exacted for injustice, because it is precisely the failure that constitutes the injustice. [Pg 169]

This is the kernel of all that is most retrograde in Mr. Carlyle's teaching. He identifies the physical with the moral order, confounds faithful conformity to the material conditions of success, with loyal adherence to virtuous rule and principle, and then appeals to material triumph as the sanction of nature and the ratification of high heaven. Admiring with profoundest admiration the spectacle of an inflexible will, when armed with a long-headed insight into means and quantities and forces as its instrument, and yet deeply revering the abstract ideal of justice; dazzled by the methods and the products of iron resolution, yet imbued with traditional affection for virtue; he has seen no better way of conciliating both inclinations than by insisting that they point in the same direction, and that virtue and success, justice and victory, merit and triumph, are in the long run all one and the same thing. The most fatal of confusions. Compliance with material law and condition ensures material victory, and compliance with moral condition ensures moral triumph;

but then moral triumph is as often as not physical martyrdom. Superior military virtues must unquestionably win the verdict of Fate, Nature, Fact, and Veracity, on the battle-field, but what then? Has Fate no other verdicts to record than these? and at the moment while she writes Nature down debtor to the conqueror, may she not also have written her down his implacable creditor for the moral cost of his conquest?

The anarchy and confusion of Poland were an out [Pg 170] rage upon political conditions, which brought her to dependence and ruin. The manner of the partition was an outrage on moral conditions, for which each of the nations that profited by it paid in the lawlessness of Bonaparte. The preliminaries of Léoben, again, and Campo-Formio were the key to Waterloo and St. Helena. But Mr. Carlyle stops short at the triumph of compliance with the conditions of material victory. He is content to know that Frederick made himself master of Silesia, without considering that the day of Jena loomed in front. It suffices to say that the whiff of grape-shot on the Thirteenth Vendémiaire brought Sans-culottism to order and an end, without measuring what permanent elements of disorder were ineradicably implanted by resort to the military arm. Only the failures are used to point the great historical moral, and if Bonaparte had died in the Tuileries in all honour and glory, he would have ranked with Frederick or Francia as a wholly true man. Mr. Carlyle would then no more have declared the execution of Palm 'a palpable, tyrannous, murderous injustice,' than he declares it of the execution of Katte or Schlubhut. The fall of the traitor to fact, of the French monarchy, of the windbags of the first Republic, of Charles I., is improved for our edification, but then the other lesson, the failure of heroes like Cromwell, remains isolated and incoherent, with no place in a morally regulated universe. If the strength of Prussia now proves that Frederick had a right to seize Silesia, and relieves us from inquiring further [Pg 171] whether he had any such right or not, why then should not the royalist assume, from the fact of the restoration, and the consequent obliteration of Cromwell's work, that the Protector was a usurper and a phantasm captain?

Apart from its irreconcilableness with many of his most emphatic judgments, Mr. Carlyle's doctrine about Nature's registration of the penalties of injustice is intrinsically an anachronism. It is worse than the Catholic reaction, because while De Maistre only wanted Europe to return to the system of the twelfth century, Mr. Carlyle's theory of history takes us back to times prehistoric, when might and right were the same thing. It is decidedly natural that man in a state of nature should take and keep as much as his skill and physical strength enable him to do. But society and its benefits are all so much ground won from nature and her state. The more natural a method of acquisition, the less likely is it to be social. The essence of morality is the subjugation of nature in obedience to social needs. To use Kant's admirable description, concert *pathologically* extorted by the mere necessities of situation, is exalted into a *moral* union. It is exactly in this progressive substitution of one for the other that advancement consists, that Progress of the Species at which, in certain of its forms, Mr. Carlyle has so many gibes.

That, surely, is the true test of veracity and heroism in conduct. Does your hero's achievement go in the pathological or the moral direction? Does [Pg 172] it tend to spread faith in that cunning, violence, force, which were once primitive and natural conditions of life, and which will still by natural law work to their own proper triumphs in so far as these conditions survive, and within such limits, and in such sense, as they permit; or, on the contrary, does it tend to heighten respect for civic law, for pledged word, for the habit of self-surrender to the public good, and for all those other ideas and sentiments and usages which have been painfully gained from the sterile sands of egotism and selfishness, and to which we are indebted for all the untold boons conferred by the social union on man?

Viewed from this point, the manner of the achievement is as important as is its immediate product, a consideration which it is one of Mr. Carlyle's most marked peculiarities to take into small account. Detesting Jesuitism from the bottom of his soul, he has been too willing to accept its fundamental maxim, that the end justifies the means. He has taken the end for the ratification or proscription of the means, and stamped it as the verdict of Fate and Fact on the transaction and its doer. A safer position is this, that the means prepare the end, and the end is what the means have made it. Here is the limit of the true law of the relations between man and fate. Justice and injustice in the law, let us abstain from inquiring after.

There are two sets of relations which have still to be regulated in some degree by the primitive and [Pg 173] pathological principle of repression and main force. The first of these concern that unfortunate body of criminal and vicious persons, whose unsocial propensities are constantly straining and endangering the bonds of the social union. They exist in the midst of the most highly civilised communities, with all the predatory or violent habits of barbarous tribes. They are the active and unconquered remnant of the natural state, and it is as unscientific as the experience of some unwise philanthropy has shown it to be ineffective, to deal with them exactly as if they occupied the same moral and social level as the best of their generation. We are amply justified in employing towards them, wherever their offences endanger order, the same methods of coercion which originally made society possible. No tenable theory about free will or necessity, no theory of praise and blame that will bear positive tests, lays us under any obligation to spare either the comfort or the life of a man who indulges in certain anti-social kinds of conduct. Mr. Carlyle has done much to wear this just and austere view into the minds of his generation, and in so far he has performed an excellent service.

The second set of relations in which the pathological element still so largely predominates are those between nations. Separate and independent communities are still in a state of nature. The tie between them is only the imperfect, loose, and non-moral tie of self-interest and material power. Many publicists and sentimental politicians are ever striving [Pg 174] to conceal this displeasing fact from themselves and others, and evading the lesson of the outbreaks that now and again convulse the civilised world. Mr. Carlyle's history of the rise and progress of the power of the Prussian monarchy is the great illustration of the hold which he has got of the conception of the international state as a state of nature; and here again, in so far as he has helped to teach us to study the past by historic methods, he has undoubtedly done laudable work.

Yet have we not to confess that there is another side to this kind of truth, in both these fields? We may finally pronounce on a given way of thinking, only after we have discerned its goal. Not knowing this, we cannot accurately know its true tendency and direction. Now, every recognition of the pathological necessity should imply a progress and effort towards its conversion into moral relationship. The difference between a reactionary and a truly progressive thinker or group of ideas is not that the one assumes virtuousness and morality as having been the conscious condition of international dealings, while the other asserts that such dealings were the lawful consequence of self-interest and the contest of material forces; nor is it that the one insists on viewing international transactions from the same moral point which would be the right one, if independent communities actually formed one stable and settled family, while the other declines to view their morality at all. The vital difference is, that while the reactionary writer [Pg 175] rigorously confines his faith within the region of facts accomplished, the other anticipates a time when the endeavour of the best minds in the civilised world, co-operating with every favouring external circumstance that arises, shall have in the international circle raised moral considerations to an ever higher and higher pre-eminence, and in internal conditions shall have left in the chances and training of the individual, ever less and less excuse or grounds for a predisposition to anti-social and barbaric moods. This hopefulness, in some shape or other, is an indispensable mark of the most valuable thought. To stop at the soldier and the gibbet, and such order as they can furnish, is to close the eyes to the entire problem of the future, and we may be sure that what omits the future is no adequate nor stable solution of the present.

Mr. Carlyle's influence, however, was at its height before this idolatry of the soldier became a paramount article in his creed; and it is devoutly to be hoped that not many of those whom he first taught to seize before all things fact and reality, will follow him into this torrid air, where only forces and never principles are facts, and where nothing is reality but the violent triumph of arbitrarily imposed will. There was once a better side to it all, when the injunction to seek and cling to fact was a valuable warning not to waste energy and hope in seeking lights which it is not given to man ever to find, with a solemn assurance added that in frank and untrembling recognition of [Pg 176] circumstance the spirit of man may find a priceless, ever-fruitful contentment. The prolonged and thousand-times repeated glorification of Unconsciousness, Silence, Renunciation, all comes to this: We are to leave the region of things unknowable, and hold fast to the duty that lies nearest. Here is the Everlasting Yea. In action only can we have certainty.

The reticences of men are often only less full of meaning than their most pregnant speech; and Mr. Carlyle's unbroken silence upon the modern validity and truth of religious creeds says much. The fact that he should have taken no distinct side in the great debate as to revelation, salvation, inspiration, and the other theological issues that agitate and divide a community where theology is now mostly verbal, has been the subject of some comment, and has had the effect of adding one rather peculiar side to the many varieties of his influence. Many in the dogmatic stage have been content to think that as he was not avowedly against them, he might be with them, and sacred persons have been known to draw their most strenuous inspirations from the chief denouncer of phantasms and exploded formulas. Only once, when speaking of Sterling's undertaking the clerical burden, does he burst out into unmistakable description of the old Jew stars that have now gone out, and wrath against those who would persuade us that these stars are still aflame and the only ones. That this reserve has been wise in its day, and has [Pg 177] most usefully widened the tide and scope of the teacher's popularity, one need not dispute. There are conditions when indirect solvents are most powerful, as there are others, which these have done much to prepare, when no lover of truth will stoop to declarations other than direct. Mr. Carlyle has assailed the dogmatic temper in religion, and this is work that goes deeper than to assail dogmas.

Not even Comte himself has harder words for metaphysics than Mr. Carlyle. 'The disease of Metaphysics' is perennial. Questions of Death and Immortality, Origin of Evil, Freedom and Necessity, are ever appearing and attempting to shape something of the universe. 'And ever unsuccessfully: for what theorem of the Infinite can the Finite render complete?... Metaphysical Speculation as it begins in No or Nothingness, so it must needs end in nothingness; circulates and must circulate in endless vortices; creating, swallowing—itself.' [9] Again, on the other side, he sets his face just as firmly against the excessive pretensions and unwarranted certitudes of the physicist. 'The course of Nature's phases on this our little fraction of a Planet is partially known to us: but who knows what deeper courses these depend on; what infinitely larger Cycle (of causes) our little Epicycle revolves on? To the Minnow every cranny [Pg 178] and pebble, and quality and accident may have become familiar; but does the Minnow understand the Ocean tides and periodic Currents, the Trade-winds, and Monsoons, and Moon's Eclipses, by all which the condition of its little Creek is regulated, and may, from time to time (*un*-miraculously enough) be quite overset and reversed? Such a minnow is Man; his Creek this Planet Earth; his Ocean the immeasurable All; his Monsoons and periodic Currents the mysterious course of Providence through Æons of Æons.' [10] The inalterable relativity of human knowledge has never been more forcibly illustrated; and the two passages together fix the limits of that knowledge with a sagacity truly philosophic. Between the vagaries of mystics and the vagaries of physicists lies the narrow land of rational certainty, relative, conditional, experimental, from which we view the vast realm that stretches out unknown before us, and perhaps for ever unknowable; inspiring men with an elevated awe, and environing the interests and duties of their little lives with a strange sublimity. 'We emerge from the Inane; haste stormfully across the astonished Earth; then plunge again into the Inane.... But whence? O Heaven, whither? Sense knows not; Faith knows not; only that it is through Mystery to Mystery.' [11]

Natural Supernaturalism, the title of one of the cardinal chapters in Mr. Carlyle's cardinal book, is [Pg 179] perhaps as good a name as another for this two-faced yet integral philosophy, which teaches us to behold with cheerful serenity the great gulf which is fixed round our faculty and existence on every side, while it fills us with that supreme sense of countless unseen possibilities, and of the hidden, undefined movements of shadow and light over the spirit, without which the soul of man falls into hard and desolate sterility. In youth, perhaps, it is the latter aspect of Mr. Carlyle's teaching which first touches people, because youth is the time of indefinite aspiration; and it is easier, besides, to surrender ourselves passively to these vague emotional impressions, than to apply actively and contentedly to the duty that lies nearest, and to the securing of 'that infinitesimallest product' on which the teacher is ever insisting. It is the Supernaturalism which stirs men first, until larger fulness of years and wider experience of life draw them to a wise and not inglorious acquiescence in Naturalism. This last is the mood which Mr. Carlyle never wearies of extolling and enjoining under the name of Belief; and the absence of it, the inability to enter into it, is that Unbelief which he so bitterly vituperates, or, in another phrase, that Discontent, which he charges with holding the soul in such desperate and paralysing bondage.

Indeed, what is it that Mr. Carlyle urges upon us but the search for that Mental Freedom, which under one name or another has been the goal and ideal of all highest minds that have reflected on the true [Pg 180] constitution of human happiness? His often enjoined Silence is the first condition of this supreme kind of liberty, for what is silence but the absence of a self-tormenting assertiveness, the freedom from excessive susceptibility under the speech of others, one's removal from the choking sandy wilderness of wasted words? Belief is the mood which emancipates us from the paralysing dubieties of distraught souls, and leaves us full possession of ourselves by furnishing an unshaken and inexpugnable base for action and thought, and subordinating passion to conviction. Labour, again, perhaps the cardinal article in the creed, is at once the price of moral independence, and the first condition of that fulness and accuracy of knowledge, without which we are not free, but the bounden slaves of prejudice, unreality, darkness, and error. Even Renunciation of self is in truth only the casting out of those disturbing and masterful qualities which oppress and hinder the free, natural play of the worthier parts of character. In renunciation we thus restore to self its own diviner mind.

Yet we are never bidden either to strive or hope for a freedom that is unbounded. Circumstance has fixed limits that no effort can transcend. Novalis complained in bitter words, as we know, of the mechanical, prosaic, utilitarian, cold-hearted character of *Wilhelm Meister*, constituting it an embodiment of 'artistic Atheism,' while English critics as loudly found fault with its author for being a mystic. Exactly the same discrepancy is possible in respect of [Pg 181] Mr. Carlyle's own writings. In one sense he may be called mystic and transcendental, in another baldly mechanical and even cold-hearted, just as Novalis found Goethe to be in *Meister*. The latter impression is inevitable in all who, like Goethe and like Mr. Carlyle, make a lofty acquiescence in the positive course of circumstance a prime condition at once of wise endeavour and of genuine happiness. The splendid fire and unmeasured vehemence of Mr. Carlyle's manner partially veil the depth of this acquiescence, which is really not so far removed from fatalism. The torrent of his eloquence, bright and rushing as it is, flows between rigid banks and over hard rocks. Devotion to the heroic does not prevent the assumption of a tone towards the great mass of the unheroic, which implies that they are no more than two-legged mill horses, ever treading a fixed and unalterable round. He practically denies other consolation to mortals than such as they may be able to get from the final and conclusive Kismet of the oriental. It is fate. Man is the creature of his destiny. As for our supposed claims on the heavenly powers: What right, he asks, hadst thou even to be? Fatalism of this stamp is the natural and unavoidable issue of a born positivity of spirit, uninformed by scientific meditation. It exists in its coarsest and most childish kind in adventurous freebooters of the type of Napoleon, and in a noble and not egotistic kind in Oliver Cromwell's pious interpretation of the order of events by the good will and providence of God. [Pg 182]

Two conspicuous qualities of Carlylean doctrine flow from this fatalism, or poetised utilitarianism, or illumined positivity. One of them is a tolerably constant contempt for excessive nicety in moral distinctions, and an aversion to the monotonous attitude of praise and blame. In a country overrun and corroded to the heart, as Great Britain is, with cant and a foul mechanical hypocrisy, this temper ought to have had its uses in giving a much-needed robustness to public judgment. One might suppose, from the tone of opinion among us, not only that the difference between right and wrong marks the most important aspect of conduct, which would be true; but that it marks the only aspect of it that exists, or that is worth considering, which is most profoundly false. Nowhere has Puritanism done us more harm than in thus leading us to take all breadth, and colour, and diversity, and fine discrimination, out of our judgments of men, reducing them to thin, narrow, and superficial pronouncements upon the letter of their morality, or the precise conformity of their opinions to accepted standards of truth, religious or other. Among other evils which it has inflicted, this inability to conceive of conduct except as either right or wrong, and, correspondingly in the intellectual order, of teaching except as either true or false, is at the bottom of that fatal spirit of *parti-pris* which has led to the rooting of so much injustice, disorder, immobility, and darkness in English intelligence. No excess of morality, we may be sure, has followed this [Pg 183] excessive adoption of the exclusively moral standard. *'Quand il n'y a plus de principes dans le cœur,'* says De Senancourt, *'on est bien scrupuleux sur les apparences publiques et sur les devoirs d'opinion.'* We have simply got for our pains a most unlovely leanness of judgment, and ever since the days when this temper set in until now, when a wholesome rebellion is afoot, it has steadily and powerfully tended to straiten character, to make action mechanical, and to impoverish art. As if there were nothing admirable in a man save unbroken obedience to the letter of the moral law, and that letter read in our own casual and local interpretation; and as if we had no faculties of sympathy, no sense for the beauty of character, no feeling for broad force and full-pulsing vitality.

To study manners and conduct and men's moral nature in such a way, is as direct an error as it would be to overlook in the study of his body everything except its vertebral column and the bony framework. The body is more than mere anatomy. A character is much else besides being virtuous or vicious. In many of the characters in which some of the finest and most singular qualities of humanity would seem to have reached their furthest height, their morality was the side least worth discussing. The same may be said of the specific rightness or wrongness of opinion in the intellectual order. Let us condemn error or immorality, when the scope of our criticism calls for this particular function, but why rush to praise or blame, to eulogy or reprobation, when we should do [Pg 184] better simply to explore and enjoy? Moral imperfection is ever a grievous curtailment of life, but many exquisite flowers of character, many gracious and potent things, may still thrive in the most disordered scene.

The vast waste which this limitation of prospect entails is the most grievous rejection of moral treasure, if it be true that nothing enriches the nature like wide sympathy and many-coloured appreciativeness. To a man like Macaulay, for example, criticism was only a tribunal before which men were brought to be decisively tried by one or two inflexible tests, and then sent to join the sheep on the one hand, or the goats on the other. His pages are the record of sentences passed, not the presentation of human characters in all their fulness and colour; and the consequence is that even now and so soon, in spite of all their rhetorical brilliance, their hold on men has grown slack. Contrast the dim depths into which his essay on Johnson is receding, with the vitality as of a fine dramatic creation which exists in Mr. Carlyle's essay on the same man. Mr. Carlyle knows as well as Macaulay how blind and stupid a creed was English Toryism a century ago, but he seizes and reproduces the character of his man, and this was much more than a matter of a creed. So with Burns. He was drunken and unchaste and thriftless, and Mr. Carlyle holds all these vices as deeply in reprobation as if he had written ten thousand sermons against them; but he leaves the fulmination to the hack moralist of the [Pg 185] pulpit or the press, with whom words are cheap, easily gotten, and readily thrown forth. To him it seems better worth while, having made sure of some sterling sincerity and rare genuineness of vision and singular human quality, to dwell on, and do justice to that, than to accumulate commonplaces as to the viciousness of vice. Here we may perhaps find the explanation of the remarkable fact that though Mr. Carlyle has written about a large number of men of all varieties of opinion and temperament, and written with emphasis and point and strong feeling, yet there is hardly one of these judgments, however much we may dissent from it, which we could fairly put a finger upon as indecently absurd or futile. Of how many writers of thirty volumes can we say the same?

That this broad and poetic temper of criticism has special dangers, and needs to have special safeguards, is but too true. Even, however, if we find that it has its excesses, we may forgive much to the merits of a reaction against a system which has raised monstrous floods of sour cant round about us, and hardened the hearts and parched the sympathies of men by blasts from theological deserts. There is a point of view so lofty and so peculiar that from it we are able to discern in men and women something more than, and apart from, creed and profession and formulated principle; which indeed directs and colours this creed and principle as decisively as it is in its turn acted on by them, and this is their character or humanity. The least important thing about Johnson [Pg 186] is that he was a Tory; and about Burns, that he drank too much and was incontinent; and if we see in modern literature an increasing tendency to mount to this higher point of view, this humaner prospect, there is no living writer to whom we owe more for it than Mr. Carlyle. The same principle which revealed the valour and godliness of Puritanism, has proved its most efficacious solvent, for it places character on the pedestal where Puritanism places dogma.

The second of the qualities which seem to flow from Mr. Carlyle's fatalism, and one much less useful among such a people as the English, is a deficiency of sympathy with masses of men. It would be easy enough to find places where he talks of the dumb millions in terms of fine and sincere humanity, and his feeling for the common pathos of the human lot, as he encounters it in individual lives, is as earnest and as simple, as it is invariably lovely and touching in its expression. But detached passages cannot counterbalance the effect of a whole compact body of teaching. The multitude stands between Destiny on the one side, and the Hero on the other; a sport to the first, and as potter's clay to the second. *'Dogs, would ye then live for ever?'* Frederick is truly or fabulously said to have cried to a troop who hesitated to attack a battery vomiting forth death and destruction. This is a measure of Mr. Carlyle's own valuation of the store we ought to set on the lives of the most. We know in what coarse outcome [Pg 187] such an estimate of the dignity of other life than the life heroic has practically issued; in what barbarous vindication of barbarous law-breaking in Jamaica, in what inhuman softness for slavery, in what contemptuous and angry words for 'Beales and his 50,000 roughs,' contrasted with gentle words for our precious aristocracy, with 'the politest and gracefullest kind of woman' to wife. Here is the end of the Eternal Verities, when one lets them bulk so big in his eyes as to shut out that perishable speck, the human race.

'They seem to have seen, these brave old Northmen,' he says in one place, 'what Meditation has taught all men in all ages, that this world is after all but a show — a phenomenon or appearance, no real thing. All deep souls see into that.' [12] Yes; but deep souls dealing with the practical questions of society, do well to thrust the vision as far from them as they can, and to suppose that this world is no show, and happiness and misery not mere appearances, but the keenest realities that we can know. The difference between virtue and vice, between wisdom and folly, is only phenomenal, yet there is difference enough. 'What *shadows we are, and what shadows we pursue!'* Burke cried in the presence of an affecting incident. Yet the consciousness of this made him none the less careful, minute, patient, systematic, in examining a policy, or criticising a tax. Mr. Carlyle, on the contrary, falls back on the same reflection for comfort in the face of political confusions and [Pg 188] difficulties and details, which he has not the moral patience to encounter scientifically. Unable to dream of swift renovation and wisdom among men, he ponders on the unreality of life, and hardens his heart against generations that will not know the things that pertain unto their peace. He answers to one lifting up some moderate voice of protest in favour of the masses of mankind, as his Prussian hero did: *'Ah, you do not know that damned race!'* [13]

There is no passage which Mr. Carlyle so often quotes as the sublime—

We are such stuff
As dreams are made on; and our little life
Is rounded with a sleep.

If the ever present impression of this awful, most moving, yet most soothing thought, be a law of spiritual breadth and height, there is still a peril in it. Such an impression may inform the soul with a devout mingled sense of grandeur and nothingness, or it may blacken into cynicism and antinomian living for self and the day. It may be a solemn and holy refrain, sounding far off but clear in the dusty course of work and duty; or it may be the comforting chorus of a diabolic drama of selfishness and violence. As a reaction against religious theories which make humanity over-abound in self-consequence, and fill individuals with the strutting importance of creatures with private souls to save or lose, even such cynicism [Pg 189] as Byron's was wholesome and nearly forgivable. Nevertheless, the most important question that we can ask of any great teacher, as of the walk and conversation of any commonest person, remains this—how far has he strengthened and raised the conscious and harmonious dignity of humanity; how stirred in men and women, many or few, deeper and more active sense of the worth and obligation and innumerable possibilities, not of their own little lives, one or another, but of life collectively; how heightened the self-respect of the race? There is no need to plant oneself in a fool's paradise, with no eye for the weakness of men, the futility of their hopes, the irony of their fate, the dominion of the satyr and the tiger in their hearts. Laughter has a fore-place in life. All this we may see and show that we see, and yet so throw it behind the weightier facts of nobleness and sacrifice, of the boundless gifts which fraternal union has given, and has the power of giving, as to kindle in every breast, not callous to exalted impressions, the glow of sympathetic endeavour, and of serene exultation in the bond that makes 'precious the soul of man to man.'

This renewal of moral energy by spiritual contact with the mass of men, and by meditation on the destinies of mankind, is the very reverse of Mr. Carlyle's method. With him, it is good to leave the mass, and fall down before the individual, and be saved by him. The victorious hero is the true Paraclete. 'Nothing so lifts a man from all his mean imprisonments, were it but for moments, as true [Pg 190] admiration.' And this is really the kernel of the Carlylean doctrine. The whole human race toils and moils, straining and energising, doing and suffering things multitudinous and unspeakable under the sun, in order that like the aloe-tree it may once in a hundred years produce a flower. It is this hero that age offers to age, and the wisest worship him. Time and nature once and again distil from out of the lees and froth of common humanity some wondrous character, of a potent and reviving property hardly short of miraculous. This the man who knows his own good cherishes in his inmost soul as a sacred thing, an elixir of moral life. The Great Man is 'the light which enlightens, which has enlightened the darkness of the world; a flowing light fountain, in whose radiance all souls feel that it is well with them.' This is only another form of the anthropomorphic conceptions of deity. The divinity of the ordinary hierophant is clothed in the minds of the worshippers with the highest human qualities they happen to be capable of conceiving, and this is the self-acting machinery by which worship refreshes and recruits what is best in man. Mr. Carlyle has another way. He carries the process a step further, giving back to the great man what had been taken for beings greater than any man, and summoning us to trim the lamp of endeavour at the shrine of heroic chiefs of mankind. In that house there are many mansions, the boisterous sanctuary of a vagabond polytheism. But each altar is individual and apart, [Pg 191] and the reaction of this isolation upon the egotistic instincts of the worshipper has been only too evident. It is good for us to build temples to great names which recall special transfigurations of humanity; but it is better still, it gives a firmer nerve to purpose and adds a finer holiness to the ethical sense, to carry ever with us the unmarked, yet living tradition of the voiceless unconscious effort of unnumbered millions of souls, flitting lightly away like showers of thin leaves, yet ever augmenting the elements of perfectness in man, and exalting the eternal contest.

Mr. Carlyle has indeed written that generation stands indissolubly woven with generation; 'how we inherit, not Life only, but all the garniture and form of Life, and work and speak, and even think and feel, as our fathers and primeval grandfathers from the beginning have given it to us;' how 'mankind is a living, indivisible whole.' [14] Even this, however, with the 'literal communion of saints,' which follows in connection with it, is only a detached suggestion, not incorporated with the body of the writer's doctrine. It does not neutralise the general lack of faith in the cultivable virtue of masses of men, nor the universal tone of humoristic cynicism with which all but a little band, the supposed salt of the earth, are treated. Man is for Mr. Carlyle, as for the Calvinistic theologian, a fallen and depraved being, without much hope, except for a few of the elect. The best thing that can happen to the poor creature is that he should be thoroughly [Pg 192] well drilled. In other words, society does not really progress in its bulk; and the methods which were conditions of the original formation and growth of the social union, remain indispensable until the sound of the last trump. Was there not a profound and far-reaching truth wrapped up in Goethe's simple yet really inexhaustible monition, that if we would improve a man, it were well to let him believe that we already think him that which we would have him to be. The law that *noblesse oblige* has unwritten bearings in dealing with all men; all masses of men are susceptible of an appeal from that point: for this Mr. Carlyle seems to make no allowance.

Every modification of society is one of the slow growths of time, and to hurry impatiently after them by swift ways of military discipline and peremptory law-making, is only to clasp the near and superficial good. It is easy to make a solitude and call it peace, to plant an iron heel and call it order. But read Mr. Carlyle's essay on Dr. Francia, and then ponder the history of Paraguay for these later years and the accounts of its condition in the newspapers of to-day. 'Nay, it may be,' we learn from that remarkable piece, 'that the benefit of him is not even yet exhausted, even yet entirely become visible. Who knows but, in unborn centuries, Paragueno men will look back to their lean iron Francia, as men do in such cases to the one veracious person, and institute considerations?' [15] Who knows, indeed, if only it [Pg 193] prove that their lean iron Francia, in his passion for order and authority, did not stamp out the very life of the nation? Where organic growths are concerned, patience is the sovereign law; and where the organism is a society of men, the vital principle is a sense in one shape or another of the dignity of humanity. The recognition of this tests the distinction between the truly heroic ruler of the stamp of Cromwell, and the arbitrary enthusiast for external order like Frederick. Yet in more than one place Mr. Carlyle accepts the fundamental principle of democracy. 'It is curious to consider now,' he says once, 'with what fierce, deep-breathed doggedness the poor English Nation, drawn by their instincts, held fast upon it [the Spanish War of Walpole's time, in Jenkins' Ear Question], and would take no denial of it, as if they had surmised and seen. For the instincts of simple, guileless persons (liable to be counted stupid by the unwary) are sometimes of prophetic nature, and spring from the deep places of this universe!' [16] If the writer of this had only thought it out to the end, and applied the conclusions thereof to history and politics, what a difference it would have made.

No criticism upon either Mr. Carlyle or any other modern historian, possessed of speculative quality, would be in any sense complete which should leave out of sight his view of the manner and significance of the break-up of the old European structure. The [Pg 194] historian is pretty sure to be guided in his estimate of the forces which have contributed to dissolution in the past, by the kind of anticipation which he entertains of the probable course of reconstruction. Like Comte, in his ideas of temporal reconstruction, Mr. Carlyle goes back to something like the forms of feudalism for the model of the industrial organisation of the future; but in the spiritual order he is as far removed as possible from any semblance of that revival of the old ecclesiastical forms without the old theological ideas, which is the corner-stone of Comte's edifice. To the question whether mankind gained or lost by the French Revolution, Mr. Carlyle nowhere gives a clear answer; indeed, on this subject more even than any other, he clings closely to his favourite method of simple presentation, streaked with dramatic irony. No writer shows himself more alive to the enormous moment to all Europe of that transaction; but we hear no word from him on the question whether we have more reason to bless or curse an event that interrupted, either subsequently to retard or to accelerate, the transformation of the West from a state of war, of many degrees of social subordination, of religious privilege, of aristocratic administration, into a state of peaceful industry, of equal international rights, of social equality, of free and equal tolerance of creeds. That this process was going on prior to 1789 is undeniable. Are we really nearer to the permanent establishment of the new order, for what was done between 1789 and 1793? or were men thrown off [Pg 195] the right track of improvement by a movement which turned exclusively on abstract rights, which dealt with men's ideas and habits as if they were instantaneously pliable before the aspirations of any government, and which by its violent and inconsiderate methods drove all these who should only have been friends of order into being the enemies of progress as well? There are many able and honest and republican men who in their hearts suspect that the latter of the two alternatives is the more correct description of what has happened. Mr. Carlyle is as one who does not hear the question. He draws its general moral lesson from the French Revolution, and with clangorous note warns all whom it concerns, from king to churl, that imposture must come to an end. But for the precise amount and kind of dissolution which the West owes to it, for the political meaning of it, as distinguished from its moral or its dramatic significance, we seek in vain, finding no word on the subject, nor even evidence of consciousness that such word is needed.

The truth is that with Mr. Carlyle the Revolution begins not in 1789 but in 1741; not with the Fall of the Bastile but with the Battle of Mollwitz. This earliest of Frederick's victories was the first sign 'that indeed a new hour had struck on the Time Horologe, that a new Epoch had arisen. Slumberous Europe, rotting amid its blind pedantries, its lazy hypocrisies, conscious and unconscious: this man is capable of shaking it a little out of its stupid refuges [Pg 196] of lies and ignominious wrappages, and of intimating to it afar off that there is still a Veracity in Things, and a Mendacity in Sham Things,' and so forth, in the well-known strain. [17] It is impossible to overrate the truly supreme importance of the violent break-up of Europe which followed the death of the Emperor Charles VI., and in many respects 1740 is as important a date in the history of Western societies as 1789. Most of us would probably find the importance of this epoch in its destructive contribution, rather than in that constructive and moral quality which lay under the movement of '89. The Empire was thoroughly shattered. France was left weak, impoverished, humiliated. Spain was finally thrust from among the efficient elements in the European State-system. Most important of all, their too slight sanctity had utterly left the old conceptions of public law and international right. The whole polity of Europe was left in such a condition of disruption as had not been equalled since the death of Charles the Great. The Partition of Poland was the most startling evidence of the completeness of this disruption, and if one statesman was more to be praised or blamed for shaking over the fabric than another, that statesman was Frederick the Second of Prussia. But then, in Mr. Carlyle's belief, there was equally a constructive and highly moral side to all this. The old fell to pieces because it was internally rotten. The gospel of the new was [Pg 197] that the government of men and kingdoms is a business beyond all others demanding an open-eyed accessibility to all facts and realities; that here more than anywhere else you need to give the tools to him who can handle them; that government does by no means go on of itself, but more than anything else in this world demands skill, patience, energy, long and tenacious grip, and the constant presence of that most indispensable, yet most rare, of all practical convictions, that the effect is the inevitable consequent of the cause. Here was a revolution, we cannot doubt. The French Revolution was in a manner a complement to it, as Mr. Carlyle himself says in a place where he talks of believing both in the French Revolution and in Frederick; 'that is to say both that Real Kingship is eternally indispensable, and also that the destruction of Sham Kingship (a frightful process) is occasionally so.' [18] It is curious that an observer who could see the positive side of Frederick's disruption of Europe in 1740, did not also see that there was a positive side to the disruption of the French monarchy fifty years afterwards, and that not only was a blow dealt to sham kingship, but a decisive impulse was given to those ideas of morality and justice in government, upon which only real kingship in whatever form is able to rest.

As to the other great factor in the dissolution of the old state, the decay of ancient spiritual forms, Mr. Carlyle gives no uncertain sound. Of the Refor [Pg 198] mation, as of the French Revolution, philosophers have doubted how far it really contributed to the stable progress of European civilisation. Would it have been better, if it had been possible, for the old belief gradually as by process of nature to fall to pieces, new doctrine as gradually and as normally emerging from the ground of disorganised and decayed convictions, without any of that frightful violence which stirred men's deepest passions, and gave them a sinister interest in holding one or other of the rival creeds in its most extreme, exclusive, and intolerant form? This question Mr. Carlyle does not see, or, if he does see it, he rides roughshod over it. Every reader remembers the notable passage in which he declares that the question of Protestant or not Protestant meant everywhere, 'Is there anything of nobleness in you, O Nation, or is there nothing?' and that afterwards it fared with nations as they did, or did not, accept this sixteenth century form of Truth when it came. [19]

France, for example, is the conspicuous proof of what overtook the deniers. 'France saw good to massacre Protestantism, and end it, in the night of St. Bartholomew, 1572. The celestial apparitor of heaven's chancery, so we may speak, the genius of Fact and Veracity, had left his writ of summons; writ was read and replied to in this manner.' But let us look at this more definitely. A complex series of historic facts do not usually fit so neatly into the [Pg 199] moral formula. The truth surely is that while the anxieties and dangers of the Catholic party in France increased after St. Bartholomew, whose dramatic horror has made its historic importance to be vastly exaggerated, the Protestant cause remained full of vitality, and the number of its adherents went on increasing until the Edict of Nantes. It is eminently unreasonable to talk of France seeing good to end Protestantism in a night, when we reflect that twenty-six years after, the provisions of the Edict of Nantes were what they were. 'By that Edict,' the historian tells us, 'the French Protestants, who numbered perhaps a tenth of the total population, 2,000,000 out of 20,000,000, obtained absolute liberty of conscience; performance of public worship in 3500 castles, as well as in certain specified houses in each province; a State endowment equal to £20,000 a year; civil rights equal in every respect to those of the Catholics; admission to the public colleges, hospitals, etc.; finally, eligibility to all offices of State.' It was this, and not the Massacre, which was France's reply to the Genius of Fact and Veracity. Again, on the other side, England accepted Protestantism, and yet Mr. Carlyle of all men can hardly pretend, after his memorable deliverances in the *Niagara*, that he thinks she has fared particularly well in consequence.

The famous diatribe against Jesuitism in the *Latter-Day Pamphlets*, [20] one of the most unfeignedly coarse and virulent bits of invective in the language, [Pg 200] points plumb in the same direction. It is grossly unjust, because it takes for granted that Loyola and all Jesuits were deliberately conscious of imposture and falsehood, knowingly embraced the cause of Beelzebub, and resolutely propagated it. It is one thing to judge a system in its corruption, and a quite other thing to measure the worth and true design of its first founders; one thing to estimate the intention and sincerity of a movement, when it first stirred the hearts of men, and another thing to pass sentence upon it in the days of its degradation. The vileness into which Jesuitism eventually sank is a poor reason why we should malign and curse those who, centuries before, found in the rules and discipline and aims of that system an acceptable expression for their own disinterested social aspirations. It is childish to say that the subsequent vileness is a proof of the existence of an inherent corrupt principle from the beginning; because hitherto certainly, and probably it will be so for ever, even the most salutary movements and most effective social conceptions have been provisional. In other words, the ultimate certainty of dissolution does not nullify the beauty and strength of physical life, and the putrescence of Jesuit methods and ideas is no more a reproach to those who first found succour in them, than the cant and formalism of any other degenerate form of active faith, say monachism or Calvinism, prove

Calvin or Benedict or Bernard to have been hypocritical and hollow. To be able, however, to take this reasonable view, one must be unable [Pg 201] to believe that men can be drawn for generation after generation by such a mere hollow lie and villainy and 'light of hell' as Jesuitism has always been, according to Mr. Carlyle's rendering. Human nature is not led for so long by lies; and if it seems to be otherwise, let us be sure that ideas which do lead and attract successive generations of men to self-sacrifice and care for social interests, must contain something which is not wholly a lie.

Perhaps it is pertinent to remember that Mr. Carlyle, in fact, is a prophet with a faith, and he holds the opposition kind of religionist in a peculiarly theological execration. In spite of his passion for order, he cannot understand the political point of view. The attempts of good men in epochs of disorder to remake the past, to bring back an old spiritual system and method, because that did once at any rate give shelter to mankind, and peradventure may give it to them again until better times come, are phenomena into which he cannot look with calm or patience. The great reactionist is a type that is wholly dark to him. That a reactionist can be great, can be a lover of virtue and truth, can in any sort contribute to the welfare of men, these are possibilities to which he will lend no ear. In a word, he is a prophet and not a philosopher, and it is fruitless to go to him for help in the solution of philosophic problems. This is not to say that he may not render us much help in those far more momentous problems which affect the guidance of our own lives.

FOOTNOTES

[1] *Life of John Sterling*, p. 153.

[2] *Latter-Day Pamphlets.* II. Model Prisons, p. 92.

[3] Letter to Mr. Carlyle, in the *Life*, Pt. ii. ch. ii.

[4] Written in 1870.

[5] The dates of Mr. Carlyle's principal compositions are these:—
Life of Schiller, 1825; *Sartor Resartus*, 1831; *French Revolution*, 1837;
Chartism, 1839; *Hero-Worship*, 1840; *Past and Present*, 1843; *Cromwell*,
1845; *Latter-Day Pamphlets*, 1850; *Friedrich the Second*, 1858-1865;
Shooting Niagara, 1867.

[6] *Positive.* No English lexicon as yet seems to justify the use of
this word in one of the senses of the French *positif*, as when a historian, for instance, speaks of the *esprit positif* of Bonaparte. We have
no word, I believe, that exactly corresponds, so perhaps *positive* with
that significance will become acclimatised. A distinct and separate
idea of this particular characteristic is indispensable.

[7] *Soirées de Saint Pétersbourg, 7ième entretien.*

[8] *Latter-Day Pamphlets*, No. V. p. 247.

[9] 'Characteristics,' *Misc. Ess.*, iii. pp. 356-358. Rousseau in the
same way makes the Savoyard Vicar declare that '*jamais le jargon de
la métaphysique n'a fait découvrir une seule vérité, et il a rempli la philos-
ophie d'absurdités dont on a honte, sitôt qu'on les dépouille de leurs
grands mots.*'—*Emile*, liv. iv.

[10] *Sartor Resartus*, bk. iii. ch. viii. p. 249.

[11] *Ib.* p. 257.

[12] *Hero-Worship*, p. 43.

[13] Carlyle's *Frederick*, vi. 363.

[14] 'Organic Filaments' in the *Sartor*, bk. iii. ch. vii.

[15] *Misc. Ess.* vi. 124.

[16] *Frederick*, iv. 390.

[17] *History of Frederick the Great*, iv. 328. See also vol. i., Proem.

[18] *Frederick the Great*, i. 9.

[19] *Frederick*, i. bk. iii. ch. viii. 269-274.

[20] No. VIII. pp. 353-371.